Charley's Columbia Backyard

By Caroline Coleman Bennett

Illustrated by Paula Hayne Bowers

Happy Exploring!
Caroline C. Bennett
2008

BACKYARD AMBASSADOR
PUBLISHING COMPANY
READER

Proceeds from sale of book will go toward promoting tourism and the Junior Ambassador Program in South Carolina's Capital City.

Dedications

To my husband and mom for inspiration, my three children for their adventurous spirits, and my dad - Charley - for being my first and truest Ambassador to Columbia.

– Caroline

To my parents and my children for their love and support, and to my husband for encouraging me to draw for myself and helping me to find my voice. I love you all.

– Paula

Acknowledgements

Special thanks go to Caroline's son Coleman Bennett and his friend Toni OgunFowora for serving as models for "Charley" and "Bernard" in the book, as well as Joy Bethea, Anne Creed and Cheryl Sigmon for their reviews and advice. Many thanks also go to those who helped jumpstart this project -- Palmetto Conservation Foundation, Carolina First Bank, Prudential Palmetto Realtors and Charlotte Berry -- and those who provided great vision and guidance -- Rep. Joe Brown, Mayor Bob Coble, Steve Camp, Marvin Jenkins, Anne Sinclair and Kit Smith.

Published by: B.A. Reader Publishing Company, 2 New Grant Court, Columbia, SC 29209 www.charleyscolumbiabackyard.com

10 09 08 07 06 05 04 03 02 01

Printed in China by C & C Offset Printing Co., LTD.

Library of Congress Cataloging-in-Publication Data

Bennett, Caroline Coleman, 1970-
 Charley's Columbia backyard / by Caroline Coleman Bennett ; illustrated by Paula Hayne Bowers.
   p. cm.
 Summary: Charley shows his new neighbor all the wonderful sights of Columbia, South Carolina.
 ISBN 978-0-9793808-0-8 (previously ISBN 978-0-9745284-5-8)
 [1. Columbia (S.C.)--Fiction. 2. Stories in rhyme.] I. Bowers, Paula Hayne, ill. II. Title.
 PZ8.3.B43757Ch 2006
 [E]--dc22
                  2006014026

Loving and Leading Your Capital City

When I was a child growing up in Columbia, my dad would take every opportunity to point out the many reasons to love our state. While driving to school, sitting on the back porch during the rain, or watching the sunset over the lake, he would often say, "Is there any better place to be than South Carolina? The weather is always pleasant, the attractions are plentiful, we're close to the mountains and the sea, and the people are so friendly. We have it all in our own backyard."

South Carolina's Capital City not only lies in the center of our state; it also lies at the center of my dad's heart. My dad is Charley, my first and truest Ambassador to Columbia.

Memories of my childhood, coupled with watching my own children explore Columbia, moved me to write *Charley's Columbia Backyard,* which Mayor Bob Coble named the Capital City's "Official Children's Book." But this is more than a book that is read once then put aside. Instead, it is a scavenger hunt for the adventurous, educational tool for teachers and parents, an informative tour guide for visitors, and – best of all – the key to becoming a Junior Ambassador.

Through a partnership with the Columbia Metropolitan Convention and Visitors Bureau and Richland County First Steps, *Charley's Columbia Backyard* has blossomed into a full-circle, community awareness initiative that includes Charley's Checklist, the Charley Pass to area attractions, the Junior Ambassadors Club and First Steps to Leadership. All of these efforts open the doors of learning and leadership to our state's youngest readers.

In this endearing story, "Charley" holds in his heart a deep appreciation for all our city has to offer and the burning desire to share it with friends and family. It is my hope, as well as the wish of the caring partners in this project, that this children's book sparks the bit of "Charley" that lies within each one of us.

Then, maybe you too will find you don't have to travel far or search deep for the greatest treasures in our country. You just might find that "It's all in your own backyard."

Happy Exploring!

Caroline Coleman Bennett

in partnership with

From his hammock swing out back
    In his Columbia backyard,
        Little Charley heard the tears and sobs
Of his new next door neighbor, Bernard.

Whatever could be troubling him
On a summer's day in June?
The sun is out, the weather's nice,
The jessamine is in bloom!

But the boy's crying continued,
And when Charley could stand no more …
He grabbed two cherry popsicles
And marched his way next door.

Handing over the ice cold treat,
Charley asked with great concern,
"What's the matter? Your bike tire's flat?
Did you get a bad sunburn?"

"No, no," cried Bernard,
With teardrops staining his face.
"Columbia's just ordinary!
There's nothing to do in this place!"

"Nothing to do in Columbia?"
Little Charley asked with surprise.
Could he have heard correctly?
Has Bernard even opened his eyes?

"Come with me," demanded Charley,
As he grabbed the boy's hand.
"Take off your shoes, come outside.
Sink your feet in the grass and the sand."

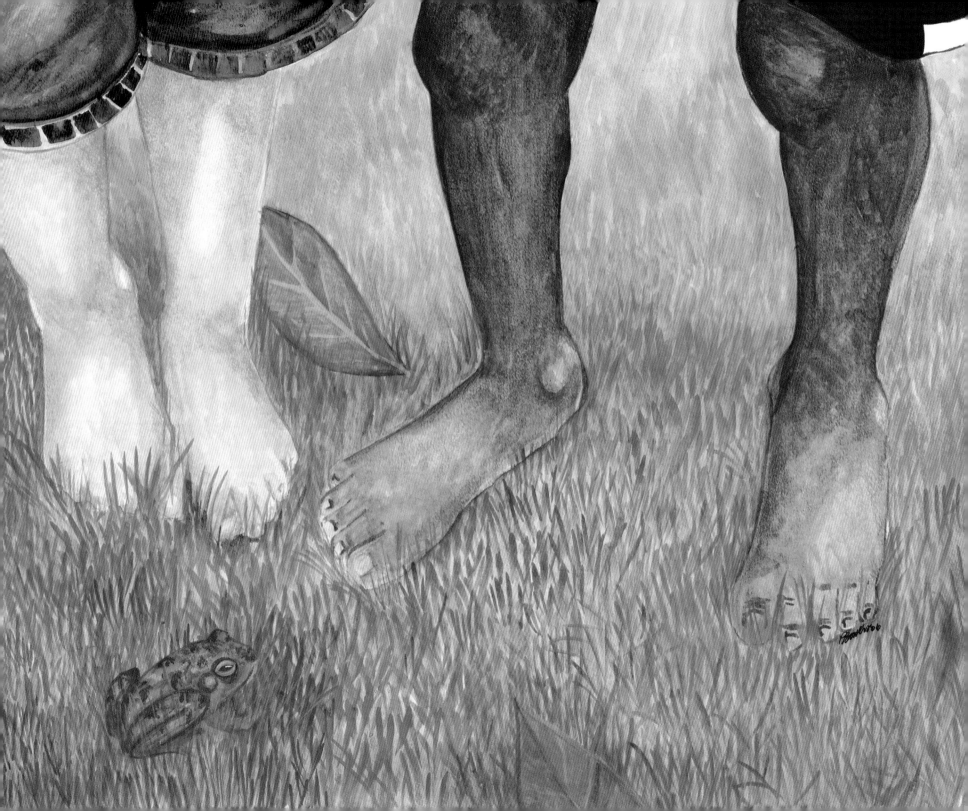

The boys walked through camellias and pines
To a tall magnolia tree.
"Let's climb up to my fort," said Charley.
But a fort, Bernard couldn't see.

For all the way up, he saw only
Knotty branches and massive blooms.
Then finally Charley straddled a branch
And said, "Welcome to my favorite room."

"Not in every city, you know,
Can you spend all day outdoors.
For in my very own backyard room
Lie treasures waiting to be explored."

"Like … have you ever caught a lizard?
Or seen a robin build a nest?
Or felt the bumpy, cold skin of a toad?
Or stuck a cicada shell on your chest?"

"Gross!" yelled Bernard with a grin,
As he let the squirming lizard go.
"And get that bug off my chest!" he screamed.
Then the laughter began to flow.

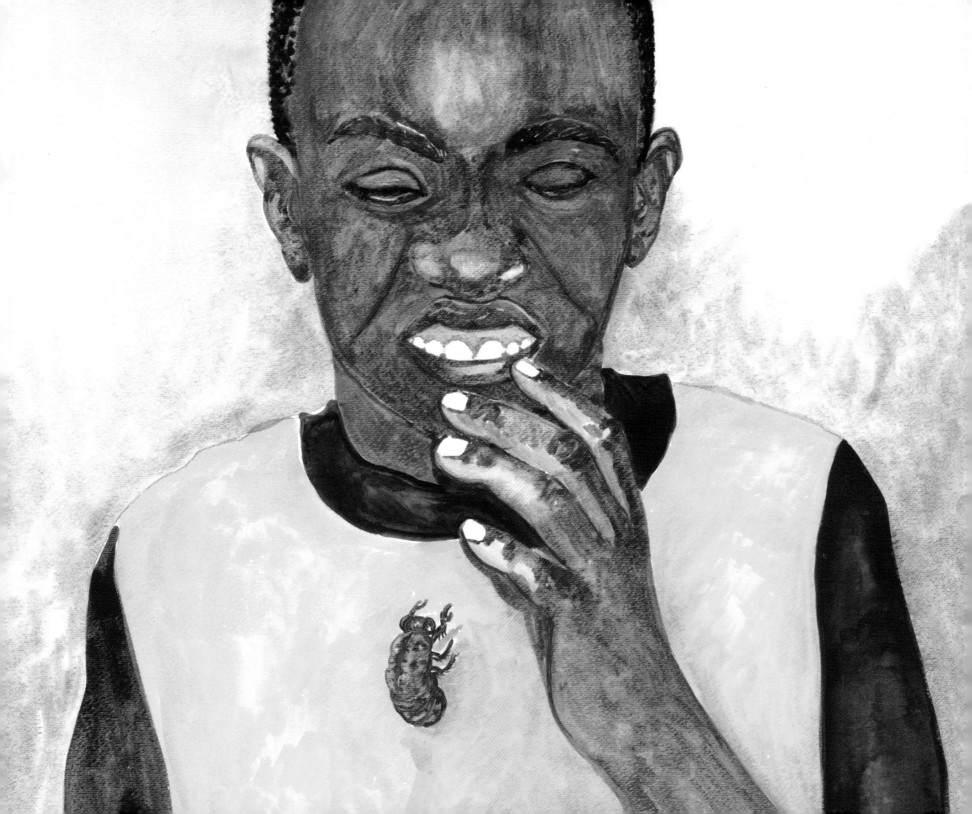

Charley said, "Have you ever felt the fuzz
Of a speckled, wiggly caterpillar …
Or witnessed the tap, tap, tapping
Of a hungry, little woodpecker?"

"No, I guess I haven't," said Bernard,
His eyes now dry and wide.
"I guess I haven't been able
To spend that much time outside."

"And listen to the sounds from here,"
Said Charley with a smile so warm.
But Bernard didn't hear any noise …
No loud cars, sirens or honking horns.

"Just listen," Charley said.
Then the faintest sounds rang clear:
The clicking of a sprinkler,
Pine straw cracking under a whitetail deer,

The faraway whistle of a train
   Rolling down steel tracks ...
   The rush of the wind through cattails
Sent chills down the boys' backs.

The sparrows, blue jays and wrens:
The medley of tunes they chirped
Sounded like an orchestra
Practicing for the night's concert.

With the whipping of an umbrella
Shading lunch on a table below,
Mom set out a feast for the boys
While they lost themselves in the show.

"Lunchtime!" called Charley's mom.
And that's all she needed to say,
For the smell of Farmers Market peaches
Was drifting up their way.

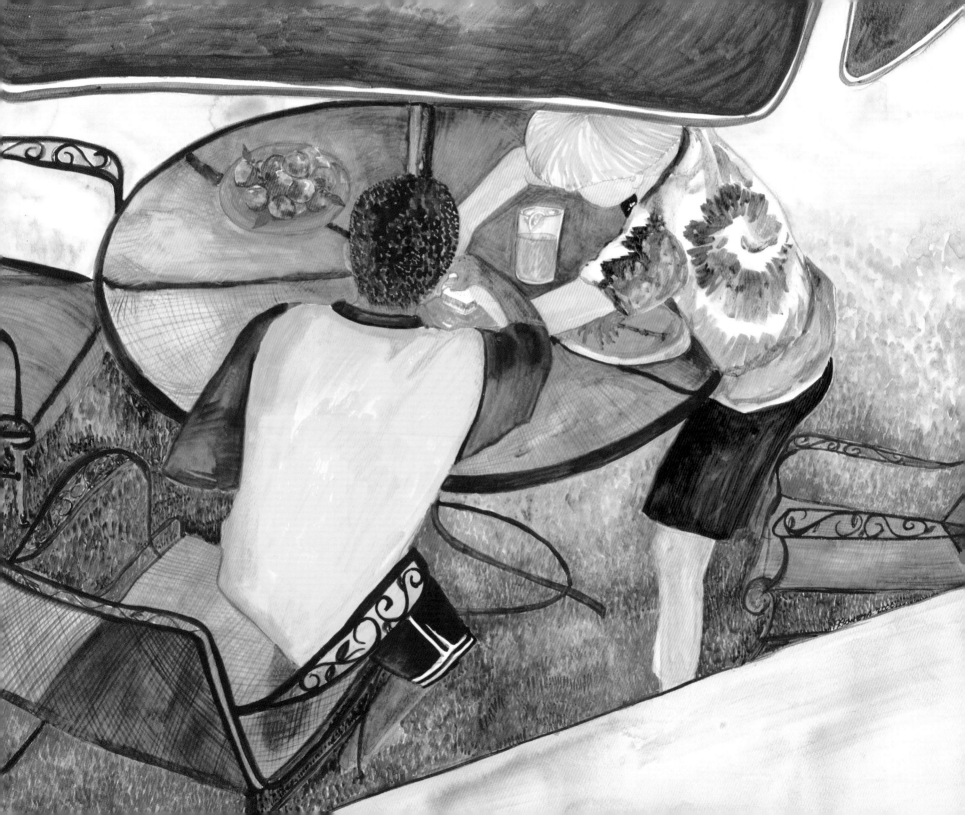

"Beyond this fence," Charley said,
  "Is a fairy-tale place, you'll see.
  Giants and castles, cannons and wild things,
A great big playground for you and me."

Bernard gave him a puzzled look.
"Believing all this is hard!"
Charley said, "Come with me. You'll see
It's all in your own backyard!"

The scenery changed like the seasons.
Charley said, "Open your eyes, your ears, your heart.
To feel the South deep in your soul,
Just let yourself become a part."

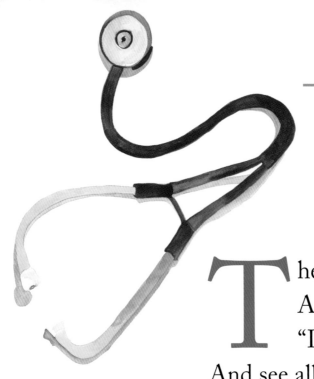

The boys became doctors at EdVenture
And worked on a patient 40 feet high!
"Let's climb up to EDDIE's™ head, slide down his belly
And see all that's inside."

"Those can't be arteries I see!"
Said Bernard with a look of doubt.
"Oh yes," said Charley, "Our city's
Children's museum leaves not a single thing out!"

"Nearby is the Marionette Theatre -
The only one in the nation of its kind.
In this castle, we'll visit knights and ogres
As each fairy-tale unwinds."

"Are those real ogres?" Bernard asked in fright.
"No, just puppets dangling from strings.
After each show," said Charley,
"You can see how they're made behind the scenes."

"But if you want more than a tale -
A story that will make you shiver and gasp -
Let's walk around our State House grounds
To learn about true heroes from our past."

The scenery changed like the seasons.
Charley said, "Open your eyes, your ears, your heart.
To feel the South deep in your soul,
Just let yourself become a part."

The boys became soldiers at the foot of a general,
Then climbed a cannon from the Battleship Maine.
"Touch these bronze faces of African-Americans
That tell a story of achievement and pain."

Charley said, "Help me hunt for the six stars
That mark where Sherman's cannons shot."
"You mean a war went on in this place?"
Bernard asked. "Surely, surely not!"

"Did you know our city has a fort?" asked Charley.
"You mean the make-believe one in your tree?"
"No," said Charley, "one with live, trained soldiers …
It's called Fort Jackson, you'll see."

A blaring bugle call startled the boys,
Then Bernard knew this wasn't pretend.
"Salute these soldiers as they march," said Charley.
"Our whole country they work to defend."

"Now, on to Riverbanks Zoo!" he said.
"It's one of the nation's 10 best.
You can see wild things from around the world,
If excitement is your quest."

The scenery changed like the seasons.
Charley said, "Open your eyes, your ears, your heart.
To feel the South deep in your soul,
Just let yourself become a part."

The boys became beasts in the jungle
Among the tigers, zebras and toucans.
Tropical birds landed right on their heads,
And a giraffe ate straight from the boys' hands.

As the boys rolled on and on,
Bernard began to grow restless.
"I need to tell my mom about all this!
I need to make a 'Charley Checklist'."

He wrote, "Go barefoot, hold a lizard,
Touch a toad, climb a tree …
Hunt for heroes, feed giraffe,
Salute a soldier, slide down EDDIE™…."

"What else, Charley?" asked Bernard.
"Remind me fast before I forget!"
Charley said, "Just keep that checklist handy.
Our adventures aren't over yet!"

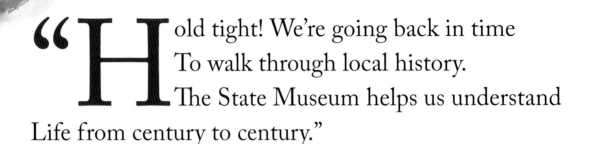

"Hold tight! We're going back in time
To walk through local history.
The State Museum helps us understand
Life from century to century."

The scenery changed like the seasons.
Charley said, "Open your eyes, your ears, your heart.
To feel the South deep in your soul,
Just let yourself become a part."

The boys trembled under the belly
Of an extinct 40-foot shark.
They dug for bones of dinosaurs
And hunted mastodons in the dark.

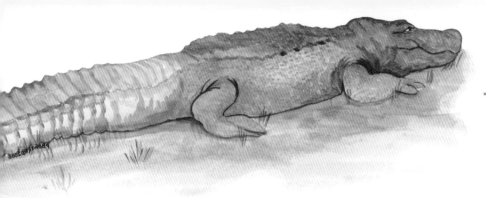

Once hunters, now hikers … they trailed on
And kayaked the Saluda, Broad and Congaree.
Soon Bernard found Columbia a most rare place
That has not just one river, but three!

On the Saluda, they stopped by a park
That's over 300 acres grand!
The explorers splashed, picnicked and played,
Then learned about plant life, first hand.

Charley led his friend to the boardwalk
At Congaree National Park.
"Look out for creatures that slither and crawl
And skyscrapers made of bark."

Blue skies turned to pink … warm air, to cool.
So many changes since the day's start.
And Bernard, too, felt something change in his soul.
Of his new home, he felt a part.

Charley said, "Tonight, let's hook a worm
At the end of a long cane pole.
We can sit on the edge of a Lake Murray dock
And pull up bream from my best fishing hole.

"And when our long day is done,
Let's watch the sun slip behind trees.
We can go to sleep to the chirps and whirs
And the gentle nighttime breeze."

Later that night as Bernard went to bed,
He cracked his window to hear the sounds.
He couldn't believe his adventures in Columbia!
What a wonderland he'd found!

From his pocket, he pulled out the checklist
To glance over it just once more.
How his day and mind had changed,
Once he met Charley, the junior ambassador.

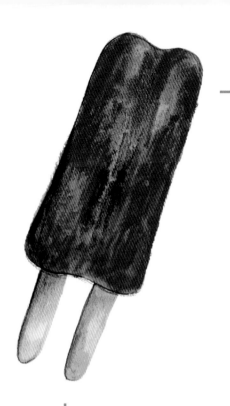

But it wasn't only the places he saw
Or the weather that warmed his skin;
It was the outstretched hand of a neighbor
That warmed him deep within.

Bernard decided that Columbia
Was just the perfect fit.
Its care for others spreads as far and wide
As the rivers that run through it.

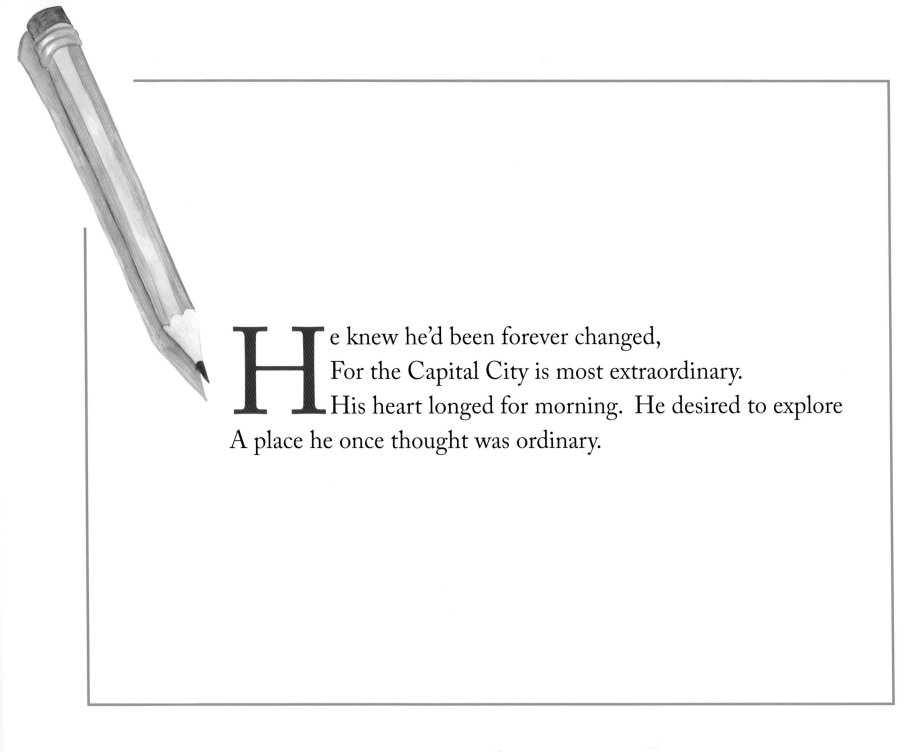

He knew he'd been forever changed,
For the Capital City is most extraordinary.
His heart longed for morning. He desired to explore
A place he once thought was ordinary.

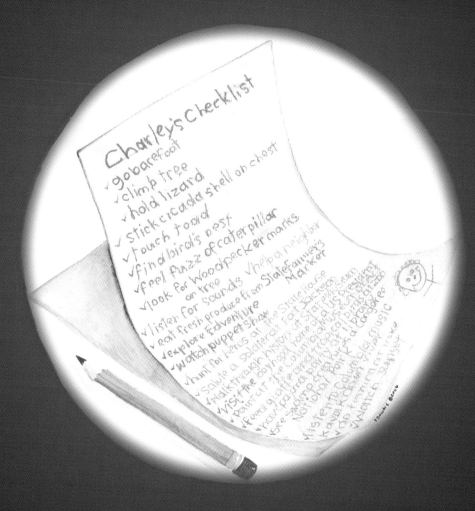

The End

Charley's Treasure Hunt

Can you find these Hidden Treasures?

Charley and Bernard love to seek and find treasures throughout Columbia. To get you warmed up for your own backyard treasure hunt, take a look again at the pictures in this book. If you open your eyes, your ears and your heart, you'll be amazed at all that comes clear! See if you can find these hidden backyard treasures in *Charley's Columbia Backyard*:

Ladybug

2 Caterpillars

2 Lizards

2 Cicada Shells

Raccoon

2 Woodpeckers

Cannon from Battleship Maine

Single magnolia leaf in grass

2 Toads

2 Pineapples (the hospitality, or "welcome," symbol)

"Junior Ambassador" badge

An American flag patch

State fruit (peach)

State flower (Carolina Jessamine)

State bird (Carolina Wren)

State hospitality beverage (iced tea)

State flag (Palmetto and moon)

2 State trees (Palmetto)

State animal (Whitetail Deer)

State butterfly (Eastern Tiger Swallowtail)

Answers provided on our website: www.BAreader.com

Charley and Bernard's Favorites

Beyond the fence of your own Columbia backyard is a fairy-tale place, you'll see. Giants and castles, cannons and wild things ... a great big playground for you and me! Take the hand of a neighbor, friend or family member, and explore Charley and Bernard's Favorites in Columbia:

Riverbanks Zoo and Garden

EdVenture

State Museum

Columbia Museum of Art

Woodrow Wilson's Boyhood Home

State House

Columbia Marionette Theatre

State Farmers Market

Saluda, Broad and Congaree Rivers

Lake Murray

Saluda Shoals Park

Fort Jackson

Congaree National Park

Finlay Park

Three Rivers Greenway

Richland County Public Library

Columbia Fire Museum

Town Theatre

Gamecock Football at Williams-Brice Stadium

Five Points

The Vista

Now grab your "Charley's Checklist" bookmark to start exploring Columbia's backyard!

For more information on Charley's Columbia Backyard, Charley and Bernard's favorites, Columbia's Junior Ambassadors Club or the Charley Pass, check out our web site: www.BAreader.com.

About the Author

Caroline Coleman Bennett is a native Columbian, who has worked in marketing, event planning and journalism in both Charleston and Columbia, S.C. The capital city has always had a special place in her heart and inspired her to create the Charley's Columbia Backyard community awareness program, which includes her children's book, the Junior Ambassadors Club, the Charley Pass and educational programs in all of Charley's hotspots. She is a graduate of Dreher High School in Columbia and Clemson University. Caroline is married to Paul (Zeke) Bennett and together they have three children: Coleman, Anna Young and William.

About the Illustrator

Paula Hayne Bowers, a local artist, was born and raised in Columbia, S.C. She specializes in painting and drawing casual portraiture of children and adults, as well as colorful landscapes. Through her love of art, Paula has opened two successful businesses – the Columbia Odyssey Art Center, where she teaches children and adults of all ages, and the ArtShack Gallery & Supplies, where local Columbia area artists display and sell their work. She is a graduate of Dreher High School in Columbia and attended Columbia College. Paula is married to Robert Bowers and together they have four children: Sarah, Alex, Evelyn Grace and Paul.